ANIMALS AT RISK !

Sea Turtles

by Rachel Grack

BLASTOFF! READERS 2

BELLWETHER MEDIA · MINNEAPOLIS, MN

Blastoff! Readers are carefully developed by literacy experts to build reading stamina and move students toward fluency by combining standards-based content with developmentally appropriate text.

Level 1 provides the most support through repetition of high-frequency words, light text, predictable sentence patterns, and strong visual support.

Level 2 offers early readers a bit more challenge through varied sentences, increased text load, and text-supportive special features.

Level 3 advances early-fluent readers toward fluency through increased text load, less reliance on photos, advancing concepts, longer sentences, and more complex special features.

★ **Blastoff! Universe**

Reading Level

Grade **K**

Grades **1–3**

Grade **4**

This edition first published in 2022 by Bellwether Media, Inc.

No part of this publication may be reproduced in whole or in part without written permission of the publisher. For information regarding permission, write to Bellwether Media, Inc., Attention: Permissions Department, 6012 Blue Circle Drive, Minnetonka, MN 55343.

Library of Congress Cataloging-in-Publication Data

Names: Koestler-Grack, Rachel A., 1973- author.
Title: Sea turtles / Rachel Grack.
Description: Minneapolis, MN : Bellwether Media, 2022. | Series: Animals at risk | Includes bibliographical references and index. | Audience: Ages 5-8 | Audience: Grades 2-3 | Summary: "Simple text and full-color photography introduce beginning readers to the threats to and protections of sea turtles. Developed by literacy experts for students in kindergarten through third grade"-Provided by publisher.
Identifiers: LCCN 2021046036 (print) | LCCN 2021046037 (ebook) | ISBN 9781644875919 (library binding) | ISBN 9781648346026 (ebook)
Subjects: LCSH: Sea turtles--Juvenile literature. | Sea turtles--Behavior--Juvenile literature. | Sea turtles--Conservation--Juvenile literature.
Classification: LCC QL666.C536 K64 2022 (print) | LCC QL666.C536 (ebook) | DDC 597.92/8--dc23
LC record available at https://lccn.loc.gov/2021046036
LC ebook record available at https://lccn.loc.gov/2021046037

Text copyright © 2022 by Bellwether Media, Inc. BLASTOFF! READERS and associated logos are trademarks and/or registered trademarks of Bellwether Media, Inc.

Editor: Kieran Downs   Designer: Brittany McIntosh

Printed in the United States of America, North Mankato, MN.

Table of Contents

Traveling Turtles

loggerhead
sea turtle

Sea turtles live in oceans around the world. Some may swim thousands of miles over a lifetime!

There are seven **species** of sea turtles.

hawksbill
sea turtle

green
sea turtle

The number of sea turtles in the
wild is dropping. Six species are
vulnerable or **endangered**.

People have caused
most of their troubles.

Green Sea Turtle Range

N
W   E
S

range = ⬛

Pollution hurts sea turtles. They often get **tangled** in garbage and fishing nets.

Sea turtles sometimes mistake plastic for food. This makes them sick.

plastic bag

Green Sea Turtle Stats

Least Concern	Near Threatened	Vulnerable	Endangered	Critically Endangered	Extinct in the Wild	Extinct

conservation status: endangered

life span: up to 100 years

fishing
net

Sea turtles like dark, quiet beaches for nesting. But people build homes and businesses along beaches. This destroys nesting areas.

Climate change also harms nesting **habitats**.

people build along beaches

nesting spots get destroyed

no place for sea turtles to nest

Save the Sea Turtles!

Sea turtles keep seagrass beds and **coral reefs** healthy. They keep jellyfish numbers down.

Without sea turtles,
ocean life would suffer.

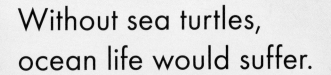

The World with Sea Turtles

1 more sea turtles

→

2 healthier sea grass beds and coral reefs

3 healthier ocean life

New kinds of fishing gear can stop sea turtles from getting caught. Special nets let turtles escape.

turtle-safe net

Certain hooks are less likely to be swallowed by turtles.

sea turtle
nest

DO NOT DISTURB
SEA TURTLE
NEST
VIOLATORS SUBJECT TO FINES
AND IMPRISONMENT

50

Governments **protect** beaches for
sea turtles. They make sure people
do not **disturb** nesting spots.

Laws make sure beaches stay dark at night.

leatherback
sea turtle

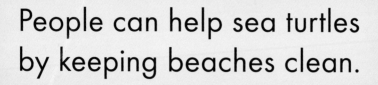

People can help sea turtles
by keeping beaches clean.

Before leaving, pack up gear and throw away trash. Knock down sandcastles.

Using less plastic keeps trash out of oceans. Cloth bags and reusable plastic are better choices.

Together, everyone can help save sea turtles!

reusable bag

Glossary

climate change—a human-caused change in Earth's weather due to warming temperatures

coral reefs—structures made of coral that usually grow in shallow seawater

disturb—bother

endangered—in danger of dying out

habitats—the places where animals live

laws—rules that must be followed

pollution—substances that make nature dirty; pollution usually comes from humans.

protect—to keep safe

species—kinds of animals

tangled—twisted up

vulnerable—at risk of becoming endangered

To Learn More

AT THE LIBRARY

Esbaum, Jill. *Sea Turtles*. Washington, D.C.: National Geographic Kids, 2021.

Gray, Susan Heinrichs. *Sea Turtle*. Ann Arbor, Mich.: Cherry Lake Publishing, 2021.

Terp, Gail. *Sea Turtles*. Mankato, Minn.: Black Rabbit Books, 2018.

ON THE WEB

FACTSURFER

Factsurfer.com gives you a safe, fun way to find more information.

1. Go to www.factsurfer.com.

2. Enter "sea turtles" into the search box and click ⌕.

3. Select your book cover to see a list of related content.

Index

The images in this book are reproduced through the courtesy of: Rich Carey, front cover, pp. 3, 5, 22; cdelacy, front cover (top back), pp. 3, 23; Vlad61, front cover (bottom back); Subphoto.com, p. 4; Isabelle Kuehn, p. 6; Marti Bug Catcher, p. 8; MOHAMED ABDULRAHEEM, pp. 8-9; pisaphotography, p. 10; travelview, p. 11 (top left); Erlo Brown, p. 11 (top right); Eliyahu Yosef Parypa, p. 11 (bottom); BIOSPHOTO/ Alamy Stock Photo, p. 12; Davdeka, p. 13 (top left) divedog, p. 13 (top right); Ethan Daniels, p. 13 (bottom); RGB Ventures/ SuperStock/ Alamy Stock Photo, p. 14; YashSD, p. 15; incamerastock/ Alamy Stock Photo, p. 16; Nature Picture Library/ Alamy Stock Photo, p. 17; Elizaveta Galitckaia, p. 18; Cmspic, p. 19; littlenySTOCK, p. 20; Willyam Bradberry, pp. 20-21.

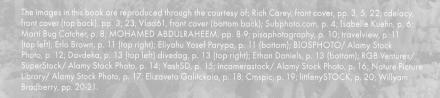